THROUGH ROSALIE COLORED GLASSES

Rosalie

A Novelette By
CARRIE J.

Illustrated By
KAMDON CALLAWAY

PAPER PEONY PRESS

For my darlings-
Scarlett, Jude, Georgiana, and Charlie,
I love you more than words can
possibly express.

We love connecting with our readers!
Email us at info@hopeandwhimsyco.com,
and a little birdie just might send a
tweet li'l gift your way...
www.hopeandwhimsyco.com

The founding literature piece of Hope & Whimsy Co's Original Book Collection, *Through Rosalie Colored Glasses* is a charming novelette about choosing kindness, cultivating true friendship, and creating meaningful community. Its beautiful illustrations, along with its classic themes and elevated tone will inspire and engage readers in later years of childhood. It is a heartwarming story that is sure to delight both young and old.

For our more eager readers we have highlighted advanced vocabulary words in pink, which are cleverly defined by Wordsmyth. All the lovely (and at times, *hideous*) pink words can be found in a small glossary at the tippy back of the book.

ROSALIE'S
HOUSE

WORTHINGTON
SCHOOL
FOR GIRLS

TABLE OF CONTENTS

VIGNETTE 1
(LATE SUMMER)

It was an unusually chilly September morning, and frost had decided to pop back in to visit after a long summer holiday. The tiny icy crystals glittered in odd patches on roofs and draped themselves across neat lawns and hedges. Puffs of smoke rose from rather startled chimneys of cozy cottages and towering townhomes. Tidy shops and bakeries that lined the cobbled streets of the sleepy town were now being perked awake by their keepers. The pale sky slowly filled up with color as it yawwwned

1

WORTHINGTON
SCHOOL
FOR GIRLS

awake, promising that there would be a most lovely First Day of School.

In the schoolyard of the town's highly esteemed Worthington School for Girls, parents and nannies stood in grim, tight clusters, seeing to the last-minute needs of their daughters or wards. Sweaters were tugged into their proper place, collars straightened, pleated skirts smoothed, and bags rechecked. A firm pat on the head signaled a final goodbye, and the children set off to grow very orderly class lines. The youngest girls seemed to be battling with gravity as they *tipped* and swayed, trying to navigate walking and waving with their coats and bulky schoolbags.

Mr. and Mrs. O'Hare stood in their own family cluster with their daughter, Rosalie. They looked quite different from the other parents in the schoolyard. They actually smiled, and warmly greeted everyone around them. However, their happy greetings were sadly not returned. Their smiles and "hellos" simply dissolved into the frosty air of the unfriendly schoolyard. Which only worsened the anxiety the O'Hares already felt for their precious daughter, Rosalie. The reason they were so anxious had little to do with sending their only child off to school for the very first time, and everything to do with the fact that their Rosalie was... well, she was different from other children. And differences were often pointed out in painful ways, were they not? They had done their very best to shield their daughter from this pain, but they often worried that they had gone about it in the wrong way.

Mr. and Mrs. O'Hare each bent and kissed their Rosalie's darling head while their own continued to flurry with worries, and doubts, and fears. Had they made the right decision to shelter her for so

long? Should they have kept sheltering her? Should they have even sheltered her at all? Was Rosalie truly ready for this? They had seriously considered sending her to Worthington for the past two years, but only last week had they finally, finally made the decision to do it. They had half-hoped she wouldn't be accepted on such late notice, but she had been!

And now... well, now they were just doing their best not to panic.

Mr. and Mrs. O'Hare held each other's hands (a bit too tightly) and tried to hide their fear with brave smiles. They watched their pulSing heart turn and wave back at them and then file, last in line, as one by one, teachers and students were each swallowed whole by the massive wooden doors of the old stone school building.

They would get their heart back at precisely three o'clock in the afternoon.

Rosalie wasn't sure how to define her feelings. She felt a constant clashing of waves inside her stomach and chest as she walked away from her parents and toward the Exciting Unknown. For what seemed like her entire life, she had let her imagination swirl about what school—a real stone-and-mortar school with other kids—would be like. Until today, she had been educated at her home in the lovely, welcoming countryside that gently rounded the outskirts of town. The way it curved around the town's edges reminded Rosalie of a lush, friendly embrace. (A hug like that sounded quite nice to her right about now.) Would she make friends at her new school? How she longed for a best friend—just like the ones she'd read about in some of her most beloved books! Books were her favorite things in life, besides her mum and dad, of course. She just wanted to learn everything—everything she possibly could—about this whole beautiful world!

She hopped along behind her classmates and teacher with a jolty spring that brought her ever closer to her very first classroom. She rather enjoyed the bumps and jabs of the other hurried, excited students because she was part of it all! School was going to be the Biggest Adventure of her life! She just felt it.

Rounding the doorway into her new classroom, Rosalie slowed her steps and then stopped to fully take in the sight of the room where her Biggest Adventure was to take place.

The room was large and bright, with a l o n g row of floor-to-ceiling windows along the entire back of it.

She slid off her hat and coat and ballooned her lungs with a deep inhale as she took in the sight of (two, four, ten, sixteen) nineteen potential new friends! And there were four very sizable bookcases stuffed full with books she'd never even seen before! (Well, no, actually. She'd read that one, and that one, and... probably nine or twenty-two others, but they were all very good.)

And her teacher! Well, she was just as pretty as a painting, with her lovely dress prim and neat and her rich henna-hued hair tidily swept back into a lovely bun.

A small squeal escaped her throat, and everyone stopped and turned to look at her. (Perhaps the squeal hadn't been so small after all.)

She felt heat slowly plume into her cheeks and rise out the top of her head as she realized forty eyes were peering directly at her.

She tilted her head shyly and gave a small wave. But the children did nothing, just continued to stare.

After an incredibly long, awkward moment, her pretty teacher stepped forward and patted Rosalie's head. "Ah, youuu must be Rosalie. I'm your lead teacher, Ms. Hoooolstein. We've, ah, heard sooo much about youuu. And are, ah, sooo very glad youuu're here, dear." She straightened, and smoothed her dress. "Now, claim a cubby to hang up your things, like a gOOood girl. Since yOuuu were registered a bit late, yOuuu will be assigned a hall locker as well, once all your uuuniforms and schOOool necessities arrive."

Rosalie felt a bit deflated. And a little numb, to be honest. (It was terrifying to be the center of attention of forty eyes!) She turned away from all the eyes and scanned the neat white row of already-mostly-filled cubbies, choosing an empty one near the end. It seemed to wave at her, asking her to make it her new home. She relaxed a little and smiled at it. She even gave it a little pat of greeting before hanging up her coat and situating her satchel, bunny, and woolen hat inside it. As she stood back, admiring how cozy her things looked there, a sharp tug of her pigtail caught her by surprise. She turned to see a lovely girl with hair of midnight satin.

"Oh, hi!" Rosalie heard herself say apologetically (even though she had not pulled anyone's hair).

When Midnight Satin Hair Girl offered no response, Rosalie stammered uneasily, "Er, my name is Rosalie—w-what's your name?"

The girl frowned at her with disdain.

"I know your name." The girl's narrow eyes narrowed even more, until they were barely slits. "Why do you look like that? Are you from another planet?"

Rosalie felt her insides shrink, as if they'd been punctured by something cold and sharp.

"W-what do you mean? Look like what?" Rosalie couldn't think what the beautiful Midnight Satin Hair Girl meant. She cast a quick look at her dress—the one she and her mum had picked out especially for this day, since her school uniforms had not yet arrived—and then down at her pretty shoes that she loved so dearly.

And suddenly, she missed her mum so fiercely, she had to swallow something balled and large way down in her throat. It felt like a big lump of sausage—the kind that Daddy burned sometimes on Saturday mornings while he flipped pancakes. And now she missed her dad! With his warm, kind eyes and strong, wrap-around-your-whole-body huggy arms.

Midnight Satin Hair Girl rolled her feline eyes, tilted her head, and studied Rosalie up and down.

"You look soooo..." She wrinkled her nose, like she was smelling something putrid. "Bizaaaarre. Your hair. It's a hideous color." She practically purred with absolute disgust.

A splash of cold spread across Rosalie's chest, fizzling out the warmth of her joy that had lived there. It then oddly changed both course and temperature as it erupted into a repeat-heat performance, involving her cheeks and the top of her head.

She looked up into Midnight Satin Hair Girl's

sneering eyes and saw herself in them. She felt she was really seeing herself for maybe the first time ever. Her long magenta hair—the hair her mum and dad were always saying was so unique, so beautiful, because no one else had ever been born with that hue—suddenly looked loud and ugly, reflected there in those slim black eyes.

Rosalie blinked back a tear and looked carefully at all her other classmates in the room.

Yes. They all—including her teacher—had suitably subdued, tastefully colored hair. Dark navy blues, rich henna browns, deep plum reds, and even a shimmery golden, over there by the chalkboard. Not one of them had bright and brash, YELLING-IN-ALL-CAPS hair, like hers.

Rosalie had always known her hair was a bit special, but not until this very moment had she realized just how "unique" it truly was. She realized, with a dull, heavy thud of punctuation, that it set her apart from everyone—and not in a good way, judging from the way Midnight Satin Hair Girl was looking at her. Such an overwhelming feeling of isolation overcame her—as if she had just been banished to live on her own iceberg. Rosalie suddenly wished to cover her head and hide herself in her soft pink blankie—the one with the ragged satin trim that was waiting for her on her bed at home.

Instead, she gave Midnight Satin Hair Girl a small smile and nod in reply, as she had no idea what to say. Midnight Satin Hair Girl, appearing to be bored with her, turned and started whispering to a small group of girls sitting at their desks. They all looked up at Rosalie with smug twinkly eyes and then covered their mouths, pretending to hide their giggles.

Rosalie walked stiffly over to an empty desk

near the back, just as Ms. Holstein called them all to attention.

School had officially begun.

At the end of that very long day, just as Rosalie had passed through the school's enormous front doors, she came to a slow halt. She looked carefully around her—searching her surroundings for several minutes—and realized something that made her stomach drop. She hadn't seen It at all that day. Not even once.

Later that day, Rosalie found herself wrapped in the loving and comforting hug of Home, with its roses blooming in the flower boxes and the air swirling fresh and green through its open windows. She could hear a lamb bleat for its mama from a nearby pasture as she cried in her own mother's arms. In between tears, she relayed the day's events: the unkind words of Midnight Satin Hair Girl (whose name, she later learned, was Vivienne Somali); the all-day whispers, giggles, and snickery side-glances

ROSALIE'S
HOUSE

in her direction; the constant jeers for bringing her stuffed bunny (only babies brought stuffed animals to school—had she brought a pacifier and bottle, too?), sitting by herself at lunch and recess, and not making one single friend.

School wasn't what she had thought it would be at all, and she didn't want to go back. Not ever again.

As Rosalie cried, she saw a flash of something she didn't quite recognize in her mother's eyes a few times, but it was quickly replaced with deep pools of hurt. As if her mother had been hurt the same way Rosalie had.

Her mother quite surprised her, though, by not saying soothing words she wanted to hear, like, "Of course, my angel. You don't ever have to go back to that awful school! And what mean ol' meanies! You don't want to be friends with people like that, anyway!"

No, she did not say anything of the sort. In fact, not only did her mother tell her she had to go back, but she also told her she must be kind to everyone— including Vivienne— and do her best to right unkindness with a compassionate heart. She explained that it took

Strength and Bravery
to choose to be
kind always
and to stand up for herself
and others
in a loving way.

And she knew Rosalie was brave enough, and strong enough, to do it and do it well.

Rosalie kept her mother's words close to her heart and found they gave her courage to face another day of school. And another, and another.

And then, on the fourth day of school, Rosalie received quite a little shock, and all her senses snapped to attention.

She saw It.

"Would you like to sit with me?"
Rosalie heard a soft voice ask her at lunch. She turned
and saw a small girl sitting alone, looking questioningly
up at her with doe-like eyes. A light spattering of
freckles graced her little nose and cheeks. She looked
to be a full year—maybe even two—younger than
Rosalie.

Rosalie's eyes lit up as she answered, "Of course—
I'd love to sit with you! I'm Rosalie."

"I'm Poppy." The little girl smiled. "I like your
bunny."

Rosalie's kind eyes crinkled.

"I like your fawn." Rosalie smiled back, indicating Poppy's darling little lunch basket that was made in the shape of a baby deer.

And Rosalie felt a bud of Hope begin to blossom.

Poppy and Rosalie sat together at lunch, and found each other at recess, every day after that. Poppy even came to play at Rosalie's house on most weekends (Rosalie was never invited to Poppy's home, but Rosalie never asked—that would have been rude). Even though they were a full class year apart, they became the dearest of friends, and that meant everything to Rosalie.

She found that true friendship
strengthened her heart,
and colored her life in the most
joyful hues.
She also found it gave her
courage.

VIGNETTE 2
(AUTUMN)

Leaves had reached the height of their full glory and were parading their new hues of deep scarlets, pale pinks, sunny goldens, and fiery citruses. They all rustled, preened, and waved at any given passerby, confident in their beauty. Wood smoke tinged the thin, clean air, sending out the promise of many snug fireside days ahead. Tucked affectionately inside the pockets and folds of coats and scarves was the anticipation of upcoming holidays and special cozy times spent with loved

WORTHINGTON
IN THE FALL

ones.

Worthington was as busy as ever in its business of challenging sharp minds and molding strong, intelligent young ladies. Afternoon science and literature classes were still being held outside on the campus's rolling, and now brilliantly shaded, lawns. Teachers and students were enjoying their last days of outdoor class time, fully taking in nature's spectacular final performance until spring! Even if it was a bit chilly on some days.

Although school had now been in session for nearly two months, Scarlett Fox had still not said one word to her new classmate, Rosalie.

Scarlett watched. She listened.

She took note of everything. It was just her way.

Constancy was what Scarlett looked for. Trustworthiness. People changed, and change could really hurt. Take Scarlett's mum and dad: they had once loved each other, and now all they did was fight. (They thought she couldn't hear, but doors and walls were only so thick.) Her dad had been taking

SCARLETT'S
HOUSE

more and more business trips, and staying away for longer and longer. She barely saw him anymore. Everything just felt different. She'd give anything to have it back the way it used to be! Her, Dad, and Mum—all together, all the time.

What she missed most was her dad showing up to all her games and regattas, and the three of them going out for dinner and ice cream afterwards to celebrate. Scarlett loved playing sports and competing, and she really excelled at it. She had shelves and shelves of trophies that proved her varied skills. However, she half-suspected that the real reason she pushed herself so hard in sports was simply to see the admiration in her dad's eyes when he watched her play. That special twinkle he'd get, recalling the key moments in the game when Scarlett had really shined, was what she practically lived for. She just adored her dad. Of course, she loved her mum dearly, too, but she just had this unexplainable, extra-special bond with her dad. And she missed him. Terribly. Although she wouldn't come straight out and admit it to herself, she was terrified that she'd lose him—that he simply wouldn't come back from a business trip, and that would be it.

So, Scarlett waited. And she watched. And she tried to read between the lines in every part of her life, as a way to guard herself—to protect herself from potential hurt.

And this guarded approach to life especially included new girls.

Yes, Rosalie looked different. And most kids loved to point out—and make fun of—differences, didn't they? Why they did this, Scarlett could not fully understand. It was cruel, and yet kids—even "nice" kids—seemed to enjoy taking part in it. Maybe it was the feeling of power and importance, thinking you were at least better than someone. Or maybe it was a warped sense of camaraderie and belonging, that you felt included, a part of something. Or maybe it was just plain relief that it wasn't you who was the target of the cruelty.

Whatever it was, it was wrong. And Scarlett was sick of it.

She had watched and noted how Rosalie handled the constant jibes.

In the beginning, the poor girl had been bombarded with them—mocked for everything from the color of her hair, to her clothes, to her bunny, to her being homeschooled, to her living in the country—nothing was off-limits. Scarlett had been certain she wouldn't last a week, but Rosalie had surprised her. She had a strength, a steady calmness, a kindness that seemed to come from her very soul. She never wavered. For every insult, she simply said, "That isn't a kind thing to say." And then she would always follow this gentle comment by saying something kind to the person—like complimenting their hair, or praising something they had done well that day.

The steadiness and kindness in her responses astounded Scarlett. And soon, the mocking and taunting had slowed. It definitely hadn't gone away completely—most kids still didn't talk with Rosalie, or sit with her or anything—but it wasn't nearly as bad as it used to be.

Scarlett was impressed with Rosalie, and the thought had crossed her mind once or twice lately that maybe, just maybe, Rosalie could turn out to be her first true friend.

Scarlett got along with many of the girls at Worthington and was probably even considered to be "popular" among them, but she found none of them to be trustworthy. The only "constant" thing about them was that they were constantly inconstant. They were up, and down, and sideways. They loved you one minute, hated you the next, and went back to wanting to be "best friends forever" the very next day. It wore on

Scarlett's nerves. She used sports as her excuse to get out of all the social activities, like sleepovers, and parties, and other nonsense. This proved to be acceptable among her peers because she was a star athlete, securing loads of wins for the school, giving Worthington a certain level of fame that made all students—even the non-sporty ones—feel special about going there. Everybody loved a winner! And it didn't hurt that she was smart, too.

Scarlett was admired, and accepted, but not connected to anyone. And she preferred it that way. But lately, she'd had a gnawing feeling that she might actually be... well, a bit lonely? She wasn't sure, but if the feeling was a color, it would be dark grey, like a weighty shadow. Rosalie, with her brightness and lightness, seemed to dispel this dark feeling whenever she was around. Scarlett couldn't deny that she felt drawn to the girl.

These were some of the thoughts swirling in Scarlett's mind when she approached Rosalie at lunch in the crowded school dining hall. Rosalie was sitting with that little girl she always sat with (Scarlett didn't know her name). There was a laughable amount of d i s t a n c e between them and all the other students—as if a large, invisible bubble surrounded the two girls. Scarlett tossed her lunch through the bubble onto the table, directly across from Rosalie. It landed with a graceless thud. She sat down without saying a word and began slowly eating her sandwich. She noted the surprised expressions on both the girls' faces but continued to eat. She took her time with each bite, and when she had finished, she carefully selected a nice firm tangerine from a fruit bowl perched in the

center of the table. Identical silver bowls of fresh fruit dotted the massive centuries-old table that stretched dowwwn the full length of the enormous dining hall. It looked more like a cathedral than a place to eat. The dining table, which could serve well over one hundred students at a time, proved its age in dents and scars. Its thick edges were worn beautifully smooth from the dining traffic of many generations of Worthington students. It reminded Scarlett of a highly polished wooden road that frequently begged her to kick off her shoes and go for a running sock slide.

She rose from the table and gave her tangerine a small toss in the air, catching it easily without looking. As she stood, Scarlett finally asked, "Are you coming to the Halloween party tomorrow?"

Rosalie exchanged another surprised look with the little girl.

"Oh! Well, Poppy isn't going, but I am. Are— are... you going?"

Scarlett nodded. "Practice is cancelled because it's a holiday." She shrugged. "See you there."

She sauntered along next to the wooden road (no sock slides today), meeting curious eyes with indifference, and tossing that tangerine.

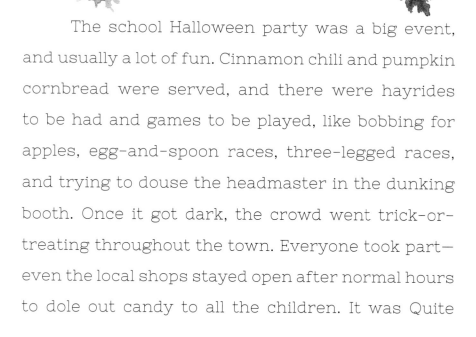 Exiting through the dining hall doors, Scarlett smiled.

The school Halloween party was a big event, and usually a lot of fun. Cinnamon chili and pumpkin cornbread were served, and there were hayrides to be had and games to be played, like bobbing for apples, egg-and-spoon races, three-legged races, and trying to douse the headmaster in the dunking booth. Once it got dark, the crowd went trick-or-treating throughout the town. Everyone took part— even the local shops stayed open after normal hours to dole out candy to all the children. It was Quite

The Event. But Scarlett couldn't seem to get excited about it this year, since her dad wasn't in town. He always ran—and won—the parent-daughter three-legged with her, and was the loudest to cheer for her victories in all the other games and races (especially when she dunked the headmaster, first try). Memories of her dad hugged nearly every nook of this holiday, and Scarlett did her best to push them aside to make room for new ones.

The early evening started out normal enough, although it was unusually warm for this time of year. Scarlett's costume felt too hot and started to itch. She parted from her mum, who was talking to a group of other mums, and meandered over to different booths, carving her way through the crowds.

While she was trying to decide between a caramel apple or a thick slice of apple strudel (the strudel was winning), a flash of bright magenta caught her eye. She immediately turned, hoping to find Rosalie. Only it wasn't Rosalie. It was someone dressed up like her in the most garish way possible. A wig of long, spiky pigtails had been created in the exact hue of Rosalie's hair, only about ten times bigger. The pigtails sprouted out of a huge round mask, again about ten times too big for the small body of the wearer, with large holes cut out for the eyes, lending a monstrous creepiness to the costume. The hideous ensemble was made complete with an outdated, raggedy faded-pink dress meant to add more insult. The whole effect was grotesque—in more ways than one.

A group had gathered around this repulsive version of Rosalie, all laughing and commenting on what a "brilliant costume" it was, and how it was "soooo realistic," hahaha, and so on.

Scarlett felt time slow as she lifted her gaze beyond the sneering group, her eyes catching sight

of a bright light—no, it was Rosalie—approaching. She watched as surprise flickered in Rosalie's eyes, and then understanding of the situation shadowed and sagged her pretty features down to her shoulders and body. It was as if a magnetic force was pulling her down, down into the earth.

And then the group saw her. First one, then two, and then the whole cackling lot turned and started pointing at her, laughing even harder.

Rosalie stood very still for a long moment. She looked so sweet—sweeter and more innocent than anything Scarlett had ever seen—standing there in her bunny costume, with those eyes. Those kind, calm eyes that then ducked

to the ground and turned away, her brightness soon swallowed whole by the thickness of the crowd.

Scarlett felt her chest ache and squeeze. She then felt something powerful surge through her body, as if her circulatory system had just received an electric charge.

She made an immediate, but firm decision. Right then and there.

Scarlett strode purposefully, evenly up to the distorted "Rosalie" and peered through those large black cutout eyes into a pair of surprised narrow ones she recognized immediately.

"You should be ashamed," she said slowly. She turned to the still-snickering group and repeated, "You should all feel ashamed for what you're doing."

The group quieted in ripples.

"Why is this funny to you?" Her voice was clear and strong, but still remained calm. "Why? Why is being so cruel so funny to you?"

She looked each one of them fully in their eyes,

only detecting slight remorse in some.

"What has Rosalie ever done to you to receive such daily cruelty from you? And I do mean daily."

She looked pointedly at Vivienne, the one behind the Rosalie mask.

"She has been nothing but kind to you all."

Scarlett pulled her costume hat off. Her long plum-red hair caught the falling rays of the sun and looked ablaze—almost as fiery as her eyes. "Yes, Rosalie is different. But it isn't her hair color that makes her different from us,

She is different
because she is always kind.
She is loving.
She is brave."

Scarlett was surprised to feel tears prick her eyes as she realized something.

"And we have all been cruel to her... whether we were actively being so, or were watching silently as others were. Doing nothing to stop it."

Scarlett looked down as that realization fully saturated.

She asked softly, "Is that really who we are? Who we want to be?"

Scarlett looked questioningly at each girl once more and then shook her head.

"I know I don't. I will take no part in cruelty."

Scarlett then walked straight toward the middle of the surprised group of girls. Although snorts and snickers were already starting to bubble up again, the girls quickly parted to get out of her way.

As Scarlett strode through, intending to follow Rosalie's exact footsteps, a familiar lanky frame standing at the edge of the crowd made her stop short.

"Dad!" Scarlett let out a surprised gush of air. Never had she seen her dad's eyes look the way they did right now. They were shining with powerful emotions that Scarlett couldn't quite place.

Mr. Fox was looking at her as if he was seeing her for the very first time. Because he was, she suddenly realized. He was seeing the Real Scarlett—Brave, Loyal, and True. She wasn't hiding behind that thick guarded wall anymore, but was becoming the courageous Scarlett she was always meant to be. She could feel the change inside her—actually physically feel it.

Mr. Fox's arms were folded across his chest as he regarded her for a moment, his lips slightly pursed, working out a thought. He ducked his head briefly and then looked her straight in the eye.

"You did good out there." His voice was light and lilting, but his eyes became serious and intense. His voice deepened. "I'm proud of you, Scarlett. And..." His eyes moistened, and his voice thickened. "And I'm... inspired by you. Your courage. Truly." He gave a nod that was a kind of salute.

Scarlett felt her spirit rise and inflate her body like a helium balloon. She leapt over to him and hugged him tight, causing the neighboring crowd to take notice.

People—especially the girls and ladies at her school—always took notice of her dad. He was uncommonly handsome, and Scarlett was quite proud of this fact. He was tall and lithe, his movements always easy, assured, agile. He had clean-cut dark hair, eyes that always seemed to hold a secret joke, and an endearing boyish grin.

Scarlett noted how the smirks of the nearby girl group immediately slid away from their features as they took notice of her dad standing there. Backs immediately straightened, mouths gaped, and eyes glazed with a swoony, dreamy quality.

Scarlett tried not to laugh.

Her dad gently set her down and then gallantly nodded to the gawking group of girls.

"Ladies." He added a chivalrous bow, gave

them each a meaningful look, and then flashed that charming grin of his.

The girls fidgeted and giggled nervously in reply.

Mr. Fox then offered Scarlett the crook of his arm, and with an exaggerated air he asked her, "Shall we go find Rosalie and her dad, if he's here? And dare them to challenge us to a three-legged?" He winked at his daughter.

Scarlett laughed and felt she could not possibly love her dad any more than she did at that very moment.

They soon found Rosalie and posed their dare to her and Mr. O'Hare, which the father-daughter duo happily accepted.

And so it was that the Foxes lost their very first three-legged race to the triumphant O'Hares. Scarlett knew her dad tripped her up on purpose as they neared the finish line, and she gladly let herself fall on top of him. They laughed so hard! And they happily congratulated a beaming Rosalie and her proud papa on their blue-ribbon win.

Not wanting the evening to end, they all decided to go trick-or-treating together. Their mums joined them, too, adding bubbly friendly

THE
VILLAGE

chatter, while the girls stuffed themselves full of their candy loot. Scarlett's heart warmed when she saw her father take hold of her mother's hand as they walked through the town's lamplit streets. Pure pleasure bloomed in her mum's cheeks and added a merry sparkle to her pretty eyes. It was a perfect night. They all had such fun! And were enjoying each other's company so much that the Foxes invited the O'Hares to their home for late-night cider, popcorn, and laughs and games by the fire.

The meaning of true friendship embraced the two families that night and would connect them tightly together for always.

VIGNETTE 3
(WINTER)

Vivienne Somali sat curled in a plushy window seat inside her family's large, elaborate library, watching the snow fall gently outside. It looked as if huge cotton balls were dropping from the sky. It was the heavy kind of snow that blanketed the ground in a matter of minutes—erasing everything dull, dark, and dreary. Such a beautiful sight should've made her smile, but she wasn't actually seeing the beauty the snow was creating. She was deep in thought, her eyebrows pulled, her mouth tight. She looked like a tiny tense kitten, silhouetted there in the center of the towering window, framed by miles of sapphire velvet drapes.

She clenched her jaw. Had she felt a twinge or two of guilt during Scarlett's preachy speech, all those weeks ago on Halloween? Or felt a dull pang when she'd watched Scarlett sit and walk around with that magenta freak and her little runt friend every day at school since then? Maybe a tiny one. Okay, maybe... maybe a lot bigger than that. And maybe she'd thought about her... somewhat questionable actions toward Rosalie every single day since Halloween. And if she was being quite honest, she'd probably even thought about it when she'd made the choice to create the costume, or when she'd singled Rosalie out on that very first day of school (which, honestly, wasn't that hard to do— her hair easily did that on its own, did it not?).

Vivienne remembered every detail of that first day of school. She had spotted Rosalie in the schoolyard right away. She'd already known who she

was, though she'd never spoken to the girl. She'd seen Rosalie many times over the years when she'd come into town—always with her parents—for shopping, or a bite to eat, or something of the sort. Ever since she was old enough to remember, Vivienne had heard her nanny gossip with other nannies and mums about how strange that Rosalie girl was. And how disturbing it was that her parents kept her "locked away" with them in that country bubble of theirs.

As a young child, Vivienne used to dream about how wonderful that might be! To have parents that hid away with her, and that spent loads of time with her, and only her, in a little countryside bubble world. To be their center of attention. To be loved, and treasured, and special, and important to them...

Vivienne's real, non-bubble world couldn't have been more different. Her parents were always rushing, rushing, rushing off to some terribly important event, or preparing for some terribly important trip, or finishing something terribly important for work. Sooo many, many Importants in their lives. There was simply no room or time for their daughters to be included as two of their Importants.

It was just the way things were, and always had been. And always would be.

Vivienne thought of her baby sister, Georgiana—

"Georgie," she called her—and her face instantly softened. How she loved her so! Upon the arrival of Georgie, Vivienne had at last felt a connection to someone. It was as if she could finally pour out all the love she had filed away and stored inside her heart since her own birth. It had all been meant for her parents, if they could have ever stayed still in the same room with her long enough to receive it.

Little Georgie was Vivienne's whole world. She did everything for, and with, her baby sister. She made sure that practically every waking second before and after school was spent with that sweet baby. She even scheduled her violin lessons during Georgie's nap time on weekends, so she wouldn't have to miss out on any precious sister time. Her heart positively glowed to see Georgie light up and reach for her every time Georgie saw her! She was just starting to talk and called Vivienne "Bi-bi" because she couldn't say her V's yet. She was so cute! And so little!

And Vivienne was determined
that she would feel
Special and Important,
because she was (she so was!)
to Vivienne!

It hurt her to see her parents constantly dismissing little Georgie in their rush, rush, rush, as they handed her off to Nanny so they could sign some important papers or discuss important, rushy things with their harried, stressed-out assistants. Soon they'd be brushing away Georgie's little pant-tugging hands and reaching arms, once she was old enough to try grabbing hold of their fully occupied, fully unavailable attention. Vivienne had stopped trying years ago.

And in a blink, her parents would miss it all. All those first moments of discovery and precious, bright-eyed wonder at new accomplishments.

Just as they had missed all of hers.

She wondered if her parents even knew how old she was now. She knew that all her birthday and Christmas gifts came from her parents' overworked assistants. The assistants never even tried to hide that fact, as they sat down with her exactly two point five weeks before the special occasion to jot down the things Vivienne wanted. The cards were even signed in the assistants' distinct handwriting.

Christmas had come and gone, and the Somali girls had spent

their entire holiday without seeing their parents even once. Oh, they had called from Paris to wish them a happy Christmas and sent them extra gifts (from their assistants) to make up for their physical absence. An important meeting popped up, darling... Very important people, you know...

It had been just as well. Her parents were no more present standing in the same room with Vivienne and Georgie than they were standing all the way over there, wherever they were, in Paris. She used to feel hurt and sad all the time at her parents' consistent neglect, but now—now, she just felt... angry. Perhaps angrier, now that Georgie was in their lives. She couldn't imagine dismissing Georgie like they did. Not spending time with her, holding those squishy arms and legs! Feeling that comforting weight of equal parts love, need, and vulnerability in her arms. And looking into those bright eyes, full of wonder, as she took in the world around her.

Her parents were missing it all. All the truly Important things they could never get back.

And Rosalie's parents were not—not missing one single thing, it seemed.

Though Vivienne was given literally every thing she could possibly want—a beautiful home, chauffeurs, nannies, the finest toys, the latest fashions, the latest everything—she wasn't given anything she truly needed: Love. Affection. Nurturing. Care. Time. Thought. None of those things could be bought and delivered by an assistant.

Somehow the arrival of Georgie had highlighted—in glaring neon—all the hurt, the disappointments, and neglect.

She did everything right! She obeyed all the rules, she dressed perfectly, she styled her hair immaculately, she got perfect grades, she played the violin at an expert level, she spoke several different languages fluently, and yet, she still could not turn the head of either parent.

And then there was imperfect, freakish Rosalie

on that first day of school. Her dress rumpled, her hair outrageous, her bag outdated, no talents to speak of, and her parents... both had come to drop her off. And they'd looked at her with such—such Love... like they were going to miss her, the few hours she was at school.

The sight had made Vivienne's jaw, and heart, and hands clench tight.

She had forced herself to look away, just in time to catch the backside of her nanny, who was already halfway down the street, pushing Georgie's pram. She was free of Vivienne duty until the late afternoon.

Vivienne thought she would scream at the injustice of it all. Why did Rosalie get love, and Vivienne and Georgie did not? How was that fair?

That was why Vivienne had chosen to do those hurtful things to Rosalie. And she would continue to do them, wouldn't she? There had to be a balancing, a reckoning—some sort of justice served, didn't there? If there wasn't, Vivienne thought she might actually go mad.

There was a necessary release that occurred when she succeeded in hurting Rosalie. A leveling of their worlds that seemed to soothe and dull that never-ending ache. In her head, she knew it was wrong, but her body seemed to press forward with the cruel agenda anyway, like a machine on autopilot. Vivienne pressed forward out of pure need to relieve the pain and fury that lately seemed to be growing. She could feel it seething and spreading, seeking perhaps to overtake her body entirely.

What could she do? She knew the other girls looked to her to take the lead; she'd seen it in their eyes after Scarlett's speech, asking her if it was true. Were they in the wrong? To admit that they—that she, Vivienne, was wrong would mean admitting defeat in the one area of her life where she felt she was actually winning. If she admitted Scarlett was right, Vivienne would lose, and lose big.

She'd lose ground, lose power, lose face—she would just lose, lose, lose. And hadn't she lost enough already? Hadn't she lost, and failed (how she hated that word)—in huuuge proportions—in trying to win the most basic things in life: her parents' Love and Attention?

Well. She was unwilling to lose anything else. No matter the cost.

"Bi-Bieeee!"

Vivienne jumped slightly at the high-pitched squeal. She immediately felt the dark intensity of her thoughts vaporize into a thin mist behind her at the sight of Nanny bringing Georgie into the library.

Georgie still had faint red marks on one cheek from her nap, and her hair was curling up wildly on one side. Her arms were already reaching for Vivienne from all the way across the room, and Vivienne felt her jaw, shoulders, and stomach relax as she skipped over to scoop her baby sister into her arms. She hugged her up, and nestled her face into Georgie's warm, squishy cheeks. She felt a wonderful, lovely peace settle and warm her heart. Vivienne spun Georgie around the room, dancing with her, tickling her, and smiling with genuine pleasure when Georgie giggled at all her varied attempts. She was careful to make sure Georgie didn't go anywhere near the fire that was steadily roaring in the library's enormous fireplace, but she let her have free rein to crawl everywhere else. And Georgie took full advantage of this freedom. She pulled books off every shelf she could reach, noisily clanged bookends together, along with ridiculously expensive knickknacks, and did so with complete delight. After Georgie had had her fill of tearing up the library, Vivienne took her to one of the window seats and watched the look on her baby sister's face transform to one of awe as Vivienne pointed at the still-falling snow.

"That's snow, Georgie—S n O W !" Vivienne explained with a merry smile.

Then her face brightened with a sudden idea.

"You want to go
play in it
with me?"

Georgie blinked and looked at Vivienne expectantly.

"Let's go." Vivienne kissed Georgie on the top of her head and got Nanny to help them get properly bundled for their snow adventure.

Vivienne carried Georgie everywhere outside, showing her all that snow had to offer: what it looked like close up, what it felt like with mittens off (for just a minute, anyway), what it tasted like with their mouths opened wide up to the sky, what it sounded like when they brought their voices down to a hushed whisper, and what it felt like to twirl in. Georgie was mesmerized, and delighted, of course, but Vivienne was sure it could not compare to the joy she herself felt, getting to experience all these things with her little sister—her family.

The two girls ended their blustery adventure with hot cocoa by the fire in the kitchen. Georgie's version of "hot cocoa" was a marshmallow dipped in Vivienne's own mug and carefully cooled. Georgie's eyes widened in wonder and tremendous appreciation of the new, sweet taste. She rapidly opened and closed her little baby fists—her way of asking for more. Lots more, preferably. Vivienne laughed and indulged Georgie with three more carefully-dipped-and-cooled marshmallows.

Later that evening, as Vivienne was tucking in a completely tuckered-out Georgie inside her crib (there was no need for bedtime stories tonight—despite the marshmallows!), she felt an overwhelming sense of gratefulness, and protectiveness.

She tenderly stroked Georgie's sleeping head and lightly kissed her soft, rosy cheek. Strong emotion surged and swelled inside her chest as she gazed adoringly at her baby sister's tiny sleeping form.

VIVIENNE'S
STREET VIEW

Vivienne blew Georgie one last kiss and slowly crossed the room to one of the nursery's dormer windows. Firelight gently flickered from the fireplace, casting a warm glow across plushy rugs that were lightly strewn with toys and favorite stuffed animals. Peering out of the small third-story window, Vivienne felt light and birdlike as she took in the sight of other warm glows spilling out from neighboring homes and streetlamps, slowing to rest in rose-gold pools on the snow-covered streets and sidewalks. Chimney smoke plumed from the tops of roofs, snoring out contented puffs into the now clear, calm night.

Vivienne hugged both arms around her chest as she glanced back at her sleeping baby sister.

Whatever would she do without her sweet Georgie?

She could not even think it.

VIGNETTE 4
(SPRING)

Sunshine gently reached in and tickled Poppy Roe's nose and eyelashes. It wanted to show her what a beautiful spring morning it had helped to create! Squinting her eyes open, Poppy smiled at the sunshine, taking in its helpful handiwork. She felt pleasure bloom into her cheeks at the sight of new green leaves sprouting on dancing trees. She also saw tiny pops of pink budding in the flower box outside her window. Poppy sighed contentedly and rolled over to look at the twin bed across from her

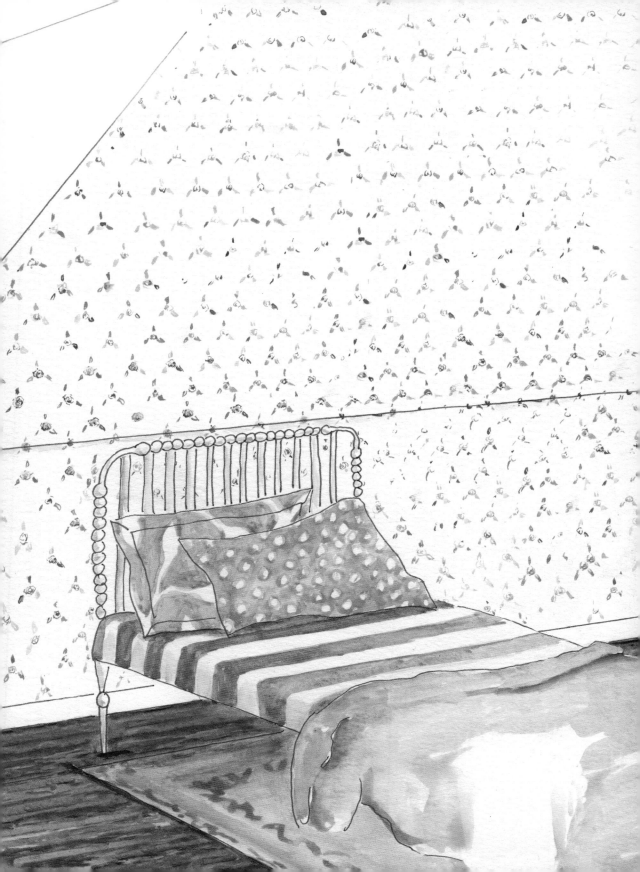

own. It was identical to hers in every way—from its spindles, to its quilts, to its inhabitant.

Her twin sister, Marigold, was still sleeping. Poppy tiptoed over to Marigold's bed and thought about tickling her awake, but seeing how peaceful she looked, she decided against it. Perhaps she'd had another rough night of it? Best to let her sleep, Poppy thought and blew her a soft kiss. She quietly crossed the room to dress for school.

Muffled breakfast noises greeted Poppy as she stepped into the kitchen. Her mother was busy flipping pancakes at the stove while her dad sipped his coffee, reading the morning paper at the table. A normal enough scene, yes, but for the eyes. The eyes told a deeper story. At a glance, her parents' eyes looked a bit blank—the typical look of the uncaffeinated parent. But if you looked further inside them, as Poppy did, you could see the weight of grief and fatigue that lived there. Dry and dull, pulling on the eyelids, and the corners of mouths. The true backdrop behind their smiling, loving ways.

"Morning, my love," her mum called softly to her, then resumed her work at the stove.

"Sleep well, my Popsy?" Her dad briefly pulled his paper down to crinkle a smile at her.

Poppy nodded. "Goldie's still sleeping."

Her dad gave an understanding nod back, and her mum, while placing various breakfast things on the table, added, "I'll check on her, as soon as I get you off to school." She kissed Poppy's head and went to grab a carafe of juice.

The three Roes ate together, casually chatting about their plans for the day. And then Mr. Roe asked a question he had asked Poppy every week for the past year: And would she be bringing a friend home to play today?

Mr. and Mrs. Roe had briefly met Rosalie a few times and thought she was absolutely lovely.

POPPY &
MARIGOLD'S
HOUSE

Poppy could see the hope in her parents' eyes that she would ask Rosalie over to their home, but this was a scary decision for Poppy, because it wasn't a decision she was making just for herself. It was a decision that involved her whole family—Marigold especially. Were they really ready for that, again?

Poppy's twin had fallen ill with a rare disease one year ago, and as a result of it, her legs had become permanently paralyzed and misshapen. While the adjustment to her new life and body had taken a tremendous toll on Goldie and the rest of the family, the Roes had been admirably strong. They were a loving, loyal family that pulled tight together to support each other through their grief at their dear Goldie's loss of one type of life... and yet, they were also steadfast in helping and encouraging her to learn how to live a new, far more difficult one. Despite their new hardships—physical, emotional, and mental—they were determined to carry on with life as they had before. Marigold continued her studies in the same class as Poppy, but because mobility was such a challenge for her, she had chosen to complete all her courses at her home for now. Worthington had graciously created a correspondence program for her, and Mrs. Roe was a shining star in helping to facilitate everything Goldie needed to stay current in it.

After spending several weeks adjusting to their "new normal" as a family, Poppy had decided to bring home one of their childhood friends to play one day. And that had turned out to be disastrous.

The "friend" had done nothing to hide her shock and revulsion when seeing Marigold's disfigured legs and feet for the first time. And it was the first time Poppy had ever seen shame in Marigold's eyes. Poppy had promised herself then and there that she would never let that happen again. And she hadn't. She had faithfully stood guard over her sister's feelings for months and months.

But as more months passed, Poppy's heart had opened little by little and had eventually found Rosalie. In Rosalie, Poppy had found a kind of friendship that soothed, and filled the gaps in her heart that had been torn by betrayal and mistrust. It was a friendship that softly shaded her life in lovely hues of grace and joy.

And a peace settled into her soul when she realized, just now at the kitchen table (with her parents still waiting for her answer), that it was Time. Time for her to be brave.

"You know... I think I will," she answered with a small smile.

Mr. and Mrs. Roe sat up straight in surprise.

"Well, well, now!" Her dad lifted his coffee cup. "I daresay, I do think that calls for a proper toast!"

Poppy and her mum laughed as they lifted coffee and juice cups alike and clinked them together.

"To Friendship!" her father said with gusto, and they all clinked again.

"To being brave," her mum said softly, looking meaningfully at Poppy. A silent message that said, "I'm so very proud of you," ticker-taped out of her loving, weary eyes and landed in a restful curl in the center of the table.

"Would you like to come play at my house after school today?" Poppy asked Rosalie at lunch that day.

Rosalie's dear face perked up in surprise. And then her eyes, catching the significance of the question, matched the honored tone in her voice when she replied, "I would love to."

Holding Rosalie's hand, Poppy led her friend through a picket fence gate that sat wedged between the stone-wall fencing of the Roes' cottage. Their home was nestled between other snug cottages on a quiet tree-lined street, just a few blocks from Worthington. Poppy was feeling confident and more at peace than she had in a very long time. It felt as if a new chapter—a wonder-filled chapter—was just beginning for the Roe family! And she let the joy of this new Hope whisk her and Rosalie right through her poppy-red front door.

Mrs. Roe was there to greet them. "You are most welcome here, dear Rosalie." Mrs. Roe's pretty face creased into a warm smile as she welcomed the girls inside.

"Thank you so much for having me," Rosalie returned with a bright smile.

"I was just about to put another fresh batch of strawberry tarts in the oven." Mrs. Roe dusted off some flour from her apron. "I'll bring some out to you girls in the garden when they're ready— Marigold is already out there." Mrs. Roe nodded toward the

The Roe's
Kitchen Nook

backyard.

Poppy gave Rosalie's hand a squeeze and led her through the Roes' quaint kitchen, with its cozy stone fireplace, old distressed beams, and cheery gingham curtains. A vase of wildflowers graced an antique wooden table that sat hugged by open windows streaming with sunlight. The warm, tangy aroma of tarts baking in the oven swirled around the kitchen. It smelled as if strawberry-scented fairies were dancing about in every corner. Mum had the top portion of the Dutch door open, so the girls had a clear view of Marigold. She was sitting with her back to them, painting on a large easel in the middle of a lush, blooming garden.

As they approached, Goldie's gaunt, shriveled legs and long, bony feet slowly became visible, as her blanket was just slipping from her lap. And Poppy's soul froze when she heard Rosalie gasp, loudly. Marigold turned, startled to see the girls.

"Your painting!" Rosalie gushed, gasping again and clasping her hands together. "It's just exquisite!

The
detail,
and the
delicacy of
the peony petals...
well, it's— it's just
breathtaking!"

Rosalie looked
completely mesmerized
by Goldie's painting, and Poppy
felt a whoosh of relief thaw her heart
and limbs.

Poppy gathered her breath and cleared
her throat. "Marigold, this is my friend, Rosalie.
And Rosalie, this is my twin sister, Marigold."

Poppy gave her friend's hand one more
squeeze and then took a few steps forward to
stand protectively behind her sister, letting her
hands come to rest on Goldie's slight shoulders.

"I'm so sorry!" Rosalie suddenly looked
a bit embarrassed. "I should've introduced

myself first, but I—I was just so taken with your work! I'm so pleased to finally meet you, Marigold." Rosalie extended her hand to Marigold and squeezed it in genuine, happy greeting.

The girls talked more about Marigold's painting, and then Poppy brought out other stunning pieces Marigold had painted.

"My goodness," Rosalie said after finishing off a second tart. "But talent does run strong in your family!"

Marigold looked intently over at her sister for a long moment and replied, "Indeed, it does. You should see what Poppy can do."

Poppy looked startled, and then her eyes dimmed as she

understood the meaning behind her sister's words.

"No, Marigold," Poppy said softly.

Marigold nodded her head firmly. "Yes, Poppy."

Rosalie seemed to take note of the sudden electric charge now sparking between the sisters. She straightened in attentiveness but continued to sit quietly.

"Has Poppy told you that she's a ballet dancer?" Marigold turned her full attention to Rosalie, ignoring Poppy's mumbled protests.

Rosalie's eyebrows shot up in surprise.

"We," Poppy interjected, her eyes downcast, her jaw tense. "We were ballet dancers. Together."

"Yes," Marigold

returned easily with a smile. "We were. But now I find I prefer painting far more."

Marigold paused for effect and then laughed an infectious, joyful laugh—her pretty cheeks a peony-pink from her joke. And then Rosalie giggled. And, finally, Poppy relaxed and gave a small laugh, too.

"Oh, Poppy." Marigold sobered with a soft sigh. "I think Mum has some dear old friends waiting for you over there."

The girls turned to the kitchen door, where Mrs. Roe was standing. A tear slid down one of her mum's cheeks, passing a soft, weary smile on its way. Dangling from her mum's graceful fingers were two red satin ballet shoes with long satin ribbons.

Poppy felt tears slide down her own cheeks and then took a long, steadying breath. She walked over to her mum and smiled, taking the shoes and cradling them like beloved pets.

"Oh, how I've missed you," she murmured to them.

And as soon as she had slipped them on, she felt wholly herself.

Fully Poppy.
Fully happy.

VIGNETTE 5
(EARLY SUMMER)

Worthington's sidewalks, meadows, and lakes were now being bossed about by new duck and goose families. Upset squawks and wing flutters let students and teachers know if they were getting too close, or were just simply in the way. A nourishing early-summer rain fell softly, deepening all the greens and floral hues around the campus. Despite the steady drops of rain, waddle and swim practice for the fluffy yellow babes didn't pause, or even slow. Oh, no, indeed! It

seemed that staying perfectly on schedule was a rule that applied to all living things at Worthington.

Standing on a neat shrub-lined path that led to the front of the school, Birdie Loon watched as a little duck family tottered right past her. A wistful smile lifted her mouth. She then turned her attention to the funneling schoolyard in front of her. Children were scurrying inside like little squirrels to get out of the rain. Umbrellas were firmly shaken off, and then neatly stored in a large bin by the front doors. Quite orderly and efficient, Worthington. Birdie's eyes scanned and landed on a pair of lovely narrow ones that were already studying Birdie- from Birdie's shimmery yellow head, down to her violet T-strap shoes. Birdie-exam seemingly complete, the intelligent, unblinking eyes vanished into a swishy arc of midnight satin.

A strong gust of wind suddenly whooshed straight through the campus, causing leaves to flutter wildly and flash their pale underbellies. The last of the mums and dads squinted out quick goodbyes and trotted off like rain-cloaked gazelles.

The bell rang, and the schoolyard was empty.

Birdie felt the warmth of her father's gentle hand glow in a circle on top of her head. Neither of them had brought an umbrella (they never bothered with those). They continued to stand there, still looking at the school, with the wind whipping about them. After a long moment, Birdie felt her father's hand move down to plant a light farewell pat on her shoulder. She listened to his footsteps slowly crunch away on the pebbled path. She could envision his loosely slung trench coat lifting and snapping in the wind, like the sail of a small boat. His striped pajama pants would cling and billow, cling and billow, playing tag with his long, lanky legs as he walked back to the small cottage they had just started renting. Despite the wind and rain, he'd walk the whole way with that easy, unhurried gait of his, his thinning blond hair all askew from sleep and weather, and his wooly slippers soggy and muddy.

How she loved her dad. She'd never known her mum, who had run off to chase some dream or another when Birdie was just a baby. (Not cut out to be a mum, she'd told her dad.) It had always been just her and him. And countless lovely towns. Her dad was a brilliant artist and regularly needed new locales to spur his genius, so they never stayed in one place long. Birdie loved their whimsical bohemian lifestyle. Her dad was her Home, and wherever they happened to live was their Adventure.

The rain started to fall more heavily, but still Birdie did not budge from her spot. Instead, she reached into her pocket, pulled out her

BIRDIE'S
HOUSE

enormous b i r d - w i n g e d sunglasses and put them on. She stayed planted there, taking her time looking.

After her yellow-gold hair had turned into a saturated dark-brass from the rain, she finally saw It through a class window.

She pursed her small mouth and then slowly walked inside the school in her calm, floaty way.

Just as Birdie was entering her new classroom, she was greeted in French with a sarcastic purr.

"News flash: there doesn't have sunshine inside."

The greeting belonged to the pretty girl with the narrow eyes. She knew Pretty Girl was referring to her winged sunglasses, which were still on her face.

Birdie was unfazed. This was not the first

time she'd been made fun of for wearing her sunglasses inside. Nor would it be the last.

A group of lovely girls gathered around Pretty Girl and half-pretended to cover giggles with dainty hands over mouths.

Birdie slowly swiveled her large, round, winged gaze to Pretty Girl. She instantly noted that the girl's name was Vivienne from the monogrammed bag she was carrying.

Birdie returned in calm, perfect French, "'There isn't any sunshine' is what I think you meant to say?"

Vivienne's smirk flattened. Her eyes narrowed and hardened into glassy obsidian.

"You look like a drowned rat," Vivienne spat in Russian.

Taking interest in the details of the classroom—

the intricately carved swirls in the ceiling were particularly lovely—Birdie slowly made her way toward the center of the room. She followed by foot the exact swirling pattern she saw above her.

Still transfixed by the ceiling designs, Birdie replied, slightly absently, in Russian, "Thank you. Rats are highly intelligent and have excellent memories." Birdie stopped, cocked her head directly toward Vivienne, and added, "And they can go without water longer than a camel."

Ignoring the snickers of sarcasm that followed her Russian remark, Birdie slowly gravitated to the far corner of the classroom. She thought she had glimpsed It over there a moment ago? As she arrived at the spot, she took note of the careful work being done by two girls.

"Your truss bridge is very well done," Birdie remarked, her words floating in the air like musical notes.

The two girls looked up from their engineering project in startled surprise.

"Oh! Why, thank you!" replied one girl breathlessly, but kindly. She flicked a long, gorgeous magenta pigtail behind her shoulder. "Are you new to our school? I'm Rosalie O'Hare, and this is Scarlett Fox."

Rosalie offered her hand, which Birdie took and then slowly dropped into a deep curtsy. Birdie didn't often curtsy, but she felt like it today. (She heard the typical affected smothered snorts behind her.)

"Ah, youuu must be our new, ah, transfer student, ah, Birdie Looooon?" a pretty woman with a tidy bun interrupted, smoothing her skirt, which didn't need smoothing. She didn't wait for Birdie to reply. "Welcome. I'm your teacher, Ms. Hooolstein. I'm afraid I, ah, hadn't had time toooo gather proper materials for

107

yOuuu, given the, ah, short notice."

Birdie detected some stress and slight annoyance in Ms. Holstein's eyes and voice, which was perfectly understandable.

Ms. Holstein continued in her prim instructional voice, "Now, dear, our class is currently applying their combined knowledge of math and physics tOOoo, ah, build a viable truss bridge. The best design will, ah, be submitted to this year's science fair! I have divided this class project up intOOoo, ah, small groups—yOuuu may join Rosalie and, ah, Scarlett, if yOuuu wish." She gave a sweeping gesture to the two girls. "They will be certain tOOoo fill youuu in on all the details, as I, ah, must gOOo gather materials for yOuuu, dear."

Ms. Holstein gave Rosalie and Scarlett a curt I'm counting on you look and then turned with purpose to busy herself with her newly added tasks.

Birdie had already taken in the bridge project at a glance and read through Rosalie's and Scarlett's calculations.

"Very impressive work. Truly," Birdie commented in her airy, absent way, indicating the girls' bridge design model. She lifted one of their calculation sheets and studied it again briefly. "Might I suggest something?" Birdie continued to study the sheets for a long moment and then looked up at both girls with a calm, patient expression.

Realizing, an awkward moment too late, that Birdie hadn't asked out of tact (and simply carried on as most people do), Rosalie quickly stammered, "Of-of course!"

Birdie blinked her thanks. "If you decrease the distance between the main support piers, here and here"—Birdie pointed to two specific places on their design—"by seven point two eight feet, you'll change the span ratio and eliminate the susceptibility of a standing wave harmonic developing when crosswind velocity exceeds fifty knots."

Scarlett's brows shot up in surprise and then settled in slightly amused respect.

"Which, as you know, is a likely velocity, given the locale you've chosen," Birdie finished, quite used to these surprised types of expressions by now.

"Um, you absolutely may suggest!" Rosalie smiled widely and gave a small laugh.

"Yes. And please, do keep

suggesting." Scarlett winked at Birdie and handed her a pencil.

Birdie was pleased. It usually took much longer to find a good flock of friend material.

The next couple of weeks flew by in bright, vivid flashes for Birdie. The memories of them permanently fixed themselves in her mind like colorful, moving pictures.

The blue ribbon and trophy win for their truss bridge submission at the school science fair. The proud, beaming faces of all their parents—

especially
Scarlett's
father—when
the headmistress
of Worthington's
elite Gifted Program
offered her praise and
congratulations to Rosalie,
Scarlett, and Birdie. (Birdie was later
told that the headmistress rarely made
appearances, so it was quite an honor that
she came, and even more so that she actually
spoke to them.)

Meeting Rosalie's darling little friend, Poppy, and her lovely twin sister, Marigold.

Cheering for Scarlett as she scored the winning goal, securing the school another championship title. Birdie wasn't generally enthusiastic about sports, but Scarlett was fascinating to watch—such skill and grace! She made it look like a form of art.

Her favorite moments, though, were the soft, slow evenings and weekend afternoons that she and her dad spent with the O'Hares, Roes, and Foxes. They went to park concerts and had picnics together. They all took part in good-natured k i t e - f l y i n g competitions and went on rowboating adventures, often stopping to lunch at one of the town's many outdoor cafés along the river. The tender image of her dad lifting Marigold in and out of a rowboat (he and Birdie were quite taken with Marigold's art, and the trio had been frequenting each other's personal studios as of late).

The warm firefly-filled evenings when Rosalie, Scarlett, and Birdie did their best to imitate Poppy's exquisite movements as they danced to outdoor concert music. And all falling -literally- quite short, in a laughing heap on the grass. Her dad and Mr. Fox cheerfully taking turns with Mr. O'Hare to push Marigold in her wheelchair, giving Mr. and Mrs. Roe a much-needed break. Mr.

Fox pushing Marigold all the way to home plate to score the winning run in an impromptu baseball game of Foxes and Roes versus O'Hares and Loons! And the gratefulness that seemed to buoy and strengthen the lovingly weary Roes. The constant physical burden of Marigold's condition shared and lightened by their kind friends.

Birdie discovered that Community and Friendship were living, breathing things. They enriched and fulfilled Life in ways simply nothing else could. And for the first time in her life, she felt roots starting to grow through the friendships she was forming. And through the community she and her dad were helping to create.

She felt the Hope
of summer beckoning them all with
warm, wide-open arms,
and Birdie decided
she was just going to let herself get
hugged into them.

Despite all these wonderful memories she'd made in just a few short weeks, it was two stage performances at Worthington's end-of-year talent showcase that impacted Birdie most.

The first was Poppy's ballet performance. She was absolutely mesmerizing onstage! She seemed to have moved like a translucent, fluid dream in those red satin ballet shoes. She looked as if she belonged in some other world, or even heaven itself. Every part of her exuded grace and poise, but something else—something much larger than all of that—was what set her apart. Joy. It seemed to spill out of her soul and into her every movement. She'd positively glowed with it, as had her parents and Marigold as they'd all sat watching her and applauding for her! The purity and sweetness of those beautiful moments was such a privilege for Birdie to witness.

And then, later that evening, Birdie had been struck by the most powerful solo violin performance she had ever heard. Vivienne's expert hands had effortlessly manipulated clear, flawless notes from her instrument. But it was the intensity and passion with which Vivienne played that had taken Birdie's breath away. Birdie became transfixed. In sharp contrast to little Poppy's joyful performance, Vivienne had seemed to play with an openly raw and deeply wounded heart. Birdie saw it in Vivienne's eyes, in her lovely hands. She heard and felt Vivienne's pain, her longing, her need. And it was at once both a sharp, powerfully angry war cry and a vulnerable wail of a child's earnest plea.

Birdie had felt her cheeks become wet with silent tears. Somehow, she understood Vivienne now. Especially afterwards, when she'd watched as Vivienne had scanned the audience with childlike hopefulness—a hopefulness that had slowly drained from Vivienne's eyes when only her nanny had come up to congratulate her. Then something else had caught Birdie's eye, just before the crowd blocked Vivienne from her view. Vivienne had scooped up her baby sister and buried her face in her chubby little neck, causing the baby girl to light up and squeal. Birdie's eyes had flickered. She had most definitely seen It.

Life was funny.

Life was hard.

Life was wholly

unpredictable.

Yet, Life was... always Beautiful

somehow—not in spite of it all,

but perhaps because

of it all?

Life wouldn't be cherished

without the Hard,

and simply wouldn't seem worth

much without the Good.

These thoughts gently swirled above Birdie's head in a revolving disk of light, just moments before Life decided to surprise with a swift Hard.

With warm early-summer sunshine spilling over the town, and only one week left of school, everyone seemed to walk about with an extra lightness in their steps. Birdie and her father were no exception, and they presently skipped and flitted with the best of them after school was let out for the day. The Loons were walking into town to meet the O'Hares, Foxes, and Roes for some tea and pastries at a lovely bakery over on High Street. Mr. Loon was wearing actual clothes today instead of his pajamas, which was probably why he was running a bit late. Birdie actually loved it when he picked her up in his pajamas, because it meant he'd had a wholly inspired day of work—no time for trivial clothing. But, perhaps pajamas were frowned upon in lovely bakeries? (In which case, a semi-inspired day was perfectly fine with Birdie today.)

The two Loons crossed a stone bridge that

offered a lovely view of the river that ran right alongside the southern edge of town. Birdie smiled, fondly remembering the rowboat excursions that had taken place here with her friends. That time when Rosalie had almost fallen out of her boat because she was so excited to spot a rarely seen rose-colored starling! Mr. O'Hare had forever lost his favorite hat in his surprised scramble to keep the boat from tipping over. The look on his face! Like he had lost an old, dear friend. Mrs. O'Hare had opened her arms, thanking the heavens—and the starling—because oh, how she had hated that hat! Made him look as if he should be out wrestling alligators, she'd

said distastefully, and how they had all laughed! Poor Mr. O'Hare had given a half-hearted laugh but looked truly forlorn about it. Which somehow made it all the more funny.

As the Loons continued to walk, Birdie cast a glance down Maple Street, a sweet, quiet lane, really, that ambled along right next to the river. Delicate shady trees and quaint lampposts neatly dotted the cobbled lane. Picket-fenced townhomes, small shops, and cafés all mixed together with casual, friendly ease. How she loved it here! Almost every café and shop along this street held fond memories of her friends—friends that oddly felt more like... her family. What a nice thought.

Having crossed two blocks north of Maple Street, the father-daughter duo rounded the corner onto High Street. It was the more upscale, elegant part of town with its tall, proud shops and its grand wrought-iron-fenced homes.

Birdie sighed deeply and contentedly as she held on to her dad's hand and took in her lovely surroundings. This very moment felt like pure, simple bliss. But unfortunately, the blissful moment was to be very short-lived. Birdie was looking up affectionately at her dad's relaxed, lopsided smile. Her eye had just flitted over to study new flecks of green paint dotted in his hair when it happened. She watched the playful twinkle in his eyes abruptly transform into alarm as he stared straight ahead. He yelled something, but what he yelled, she couldn't be sure.

For Birdie, everything suddenly seemed to move in slow motion. Sounds became muffled, as if she'd been dunked underwater. Her eyes caught the sight of flames licking the feet of a girl with midnight satin hair as she bolted from the front door of a beautiful, blazing home on High Street.

She heard her father yell something again and tear away from her hand. She noted a flash of magenta vanishing through one of the open windows of the first floor, while she heard a voice that sounded a lot like Poppy's scream,

"Rosalie! NooO!"

Terrified, begging screams seemed to be coming from the girl who had just run out of the house. The girl, Birdie realized, was Vivienne Somali.

She felt her own body wanting to heave a scream as she saw her father move toward the house, which was rapidly turning into an inferno.

She managed to move her body forward (why were her limbs so heavy?) and somehow made it up to Vivienne's violently trembling frame. Vivienne's face was contorted in tear-streaked horror, and Birdie felt herself wrap her heavy arms around the poor girl's shaking body. Birdie held her as tight as she could and looked up in time to see her father jolt to a stop in one of the flowerbeds at the front of the enormous stone home. Vivienne's soot-and-tear-stained nanny was next to him, pointing a shaky hand up high. She then saw her dad lift his arms to the heavens as fire and smoke billowed out of the open lower windows. Birdie lifted her gaze up to where he was reaching and saw magenta, hiiiigh up in a third-story dormer window.

Rosalie.

Rosalie was cradling a wailing bundle of blankets in her arms.

Birdie held her breath as she saw the little bundle release from Rosalie's arms and fall, fall, fall straight dowwwn into her father's slender but strong arms. She began to breathe again as she watched him gently hug and rush the bundle safely away into someone else's capable adult arms. Birdie realized the arms belonged to Mrs. O'Hare, who was still panting, evidently just arriving to the scene. The poor nanny crumpled into a heap at Mrs. O'Hare's feet, trembling and crying in relief.

She felt Vivienne jerk away from her and sprint toward the bundle.

Birdie searched for her father and saw him back at the same spot inside the flowerbed with his arms outstretched again, this time flanked on each side by Mr. O'Hare and Mr. Fox.

And one second, their dear Rosalie was standing there, framed in the window like a lovely flower painting, and the next second, she... she simply wasn't.

The whole house became consumed by flames and **thick black** smoke.

Birdie stood on the back steps of Worthington, which led down to a common gathering area of the sprawling campus. It was the most magnificent school Birdie had ever attended. It seemed to spread out for miles, if one included the buildings used for the Gifted Program. There were large stone dormitories, beautifully kept stables and jumping arenas, pristine sporting fields, an intimidatingly ornate auditorium, and even a towering, elegant dance hall. The school was quite extraordinary in that, despite its massiveness, its class sizes were quite small and intimate. Birdie had very much enjoyed attending here.

A gentle breeze caught and played with her dress. It was the last day of school—most likely her final day, as she and her dad were sure to leave for a new Adventure soon.

She had on her winged sunglasses, as always, but she didn't need them.

She saw It everywhere.

Up, and down, and across the campus, she saw magenta tresses. Long, short, curly, straight, frizzy, sleek—all magenta. Even her own long golden locks had temporarily taken on the shockingly magnificent hue.

Word had spread like wildfire (pardon the expression) regarding Rosalie's heroism in saving Vivienne's baby sister. And Vivienne herself had ignited it, along with the temporary hair dye phenomenon. She had been the first to show up to school sporting magenta hair in honor of Rosalie, and the next day, her whole class had dyed their hair (even Ms. Holstein!). By the third day, the entire school had taken on the beautiful, bold hue. Such a Change was seen in Vivienne! A perfect, complete brokenness distinguished her—not the kind that hindered the spirit, but rather the opposite. It was the kind of ground-leveling humility where one's spirit could start from scratch. To begin that important process of properly building, strengthening, and growing one's character. It's how Integrity bloomed. Genuine gratefulness was evident in the way Vivienne moved, and the way she praised Rosalie to literally everyone she came in contact with, these days following the fire. And this change seemed to be taking firm root inside her, which visibly impacted all those around her as well. Indeed, the mass number of magenta-hued heads Birdie now saw at Worthington was certainly evidence of Vivienne's powerful influence.

But really, Birdie knew it was mostly due to Rosalie herself. Who Rosalie was—that was what had truly sparked and spread the enthusiasm for this unified Act of Honoring.

Rosalie's unwaveringly kind,

brave,

and understanding nature

was undeniable—even to those

who had mocked her.

Birdie suddenly felt a soft glow of warmth approach from behind her.

"You see It, too, don't you?" a soft voice questioned.

Birdie smiled, immediately recognizing but not turning toward the voice. She felt the glow slowly move forward and stop right beside her.

Birdie nodded once in response.

"Your sunglasses," the soft voice continued. "Do they help you see It?"

Birdie, still looking at all the splashes of magenta dotting the campus lawn like animated blooms, said in that faraway, airy way of hers, "Yes. And no. When I put them on, I'm choosing to look for It." Birdie paused, her lilting voice gently swirling up, up toward the overhanging tree limbs. "It's quite hard to see sometimes, you know, if you're not looking for It."

Birdie took off her sunglasses and turned to her friend.

"And It isn't hard to see today, Rosalie.
Love and Kindness are blooming and shimmering everywhere."

THE END

"Love is patient, love is kind. It does not envy, it does not boast, it is not proud. It does not dishonor others, it is not self-seeking, it is not easily angered, it keeps no record of wrongs. Love does not delight in evil but rejoices with the truth. It always protects, always trusts, always hopes, always perseveres. Love never fails."

—I Corinthians 13:4–8

EPILOGUE

Birds tweeted their sweet end-of-summer tunes, jittering leaves and limbs as they flitted from the trees that lined Worthington's bustling schoolyard. Today officially marked Rosalie's second "First Day" of school here. So much had changed since last year! So many friendships forged and wonderful memories made! Rosalie felt not only a part of the school now, but a part of the town itself as well. The entire town knew about her heroism and had opened their homes and shops and hearts to her. She became a dear part of their community—a beautiful magenta symbol of Hope, Love, Grace, and Kindness for the town.

The entire Somali family, in particular, had opened their hearts wide to her. The loss of their home and the near loss of their baby girl had been a terrifying reality jolt for them all. Mr. and Mrs. Somali's "terribly importants" suddenly didn't seem so to them anymore. While they began the slow process of rebuilding their home, they seemed to be restructuring their lives as well. Busy nothings that had taken up so much of their Time in the past were greatly reduced. Their focus was now their little girls. Their family. And little by little, hour by precious hour, they began to build relationships with their precious daughters.

The Somalis had thrown an elaborate tented soiree in honor of Rosalie shortly after the fire, and almost the entire town had attended! Vivienne had apologized genuinely and profusely for her behavior toward Rosalie and had spent the entire evening of the soiree making sure Rosalie and her family were treated like royalty. Because of Rosalie, Vivienne now had everything she'd ever hoped for! And needed! And she made it widely known that she was forever grateful to Rosalie.

At one point in the evening, in a quiet corner, Vivienne had struggled to hold back tears as she tried to express her full gratitude to Rosalie for saving little Georgie's life. The depth of Love that Vivienne had for her little sister was easy to see, but Rosalie also detected something else that lived even deeper beneath that Love. Rosalie had felt compelled to gently place her hand on Vivienne's arm and say softly, but intently,

"I would have done the same for you, Vivienne."

The shock in Vivienne's eyes confirmed what Rosalie had already sensed. It had caused Rosalie's heart to break a little, as it expanded

in understanding and compassion.

And traces of a friendship
had then started
to bud
between the two girls.

Rosalie now looked across the mingling, cheery schoolyard. She spotted Marigold with the rest of the Roe family, just as Poppy started to walk toward

the same class line that Rosalie had been in last year. Rosalie hopped over to the Roes and gave them all happy hellos and quick hugs.

"Save a seat for me at lunch!" Rosalie merrily called out to Poppy as she skipped back over to the line of her own new class.

She gave her parents another wave and blew them more kisses. Their faces weren't scrunched with worry like they had been last year. (Rosalie detected only a hint of a tear in her mum's eye this time.) They both blew kisses back to her and waved, and then her mum's head settled back against her dad's chest. They'd stay to see their heart hop off, until it was no longer in sight.

Rosalie found Scarlett in line and walked up next to her.

"Ready for a new year?" Rosalie asked her beautiful plum-haired friend.

Scarlett smiled, casting a contented look back at her parents. Mrs. Fox was standing nestled against Mr. Fox with his arms wrapped around her—things

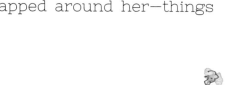

communicated, things forgiven, things mended, things set to Right. And what gave her heart the happiest lurch was seeing her dad's hand resting lovingly on her mum's smooth, slightly rounded tummy. She was going to get a baby brother, or sister, for Christmas! (She just knew it was going to be a brother.)

"I've never felt more ready." Scarlett smiled at her dear friend. "I just wish Birdie was here with us."

"I do, too," Rosalie said softly.

"I do, too," said another soft voice.

Rosalie and Scarlett turned to see Vivienne step into line behind them, with both her parents, and baby Georgie, waving happy greetings to them all.

Scarlett and Rosalie warmly returned the welcome.

Vivienne looked transformed. Her lovely face had a peaceful, contented Joy that glowed through her skin and shined through her cheerful eyes.

Hope surged through Rosalie's heart, and she

made a decision.

"The Loons are living in a little southern village by the sea now," Rosalie half-blurted, looking hopefully at Vivienne and her parents. "We're—the Foxes, the Roes, and my family, I mean—well, we're all taking a holiday trip down there for fall break. Would—would you all like to join us?"

The Somalis looked at her in surprise. Except for Georgie, who clapped her chubby hands together and squealed, "Da! Da!"

They all laughed, and then Mrs. Somali smiled kindly. "I think what Georgie meant was, we'd be honored to join all of you, Rosalie. Thank you." She reached out and squeezed Rosalie's hand with genuine gratitude.

Rosalie cast a quick glance at Scarlett, who looked so pleased with Rosalie's impromptu invitation, and she knew in her heart that Birdie, and Poppy, and Marigold would be, too.

However, she was most certain that no

one could've looked more pleased than the lovely Vivienne Somali.

Birdie was right. Sometimes you did have to choose to look hard to see the Good. But that was only one of the many choices it took to grow a Garden of Love and Kindness.

You also had to be Brave, like Rosalie's mum had told her, in choosing to be kind always. Planting those Kindness seeds so that more of It can grow. It also took a great deal of Love and Hope (and Patience, Faithfulness, Humility, Grace, Selflessness and many more hard choices) to nurture Kindness into blooming to its full potential.

Rosalie was so grateful for these Hope-filled days, because Love and Kindness truly were blooming all over her joyful town. It was turning into a caring, connected community—an extended family, really—that she, and her family and friends were helping to create.

They were all
—together—
bravely coloring Life
in the most magnificent
hues of
Love, Kindness,
Hope, Grace,
and true Friendship.

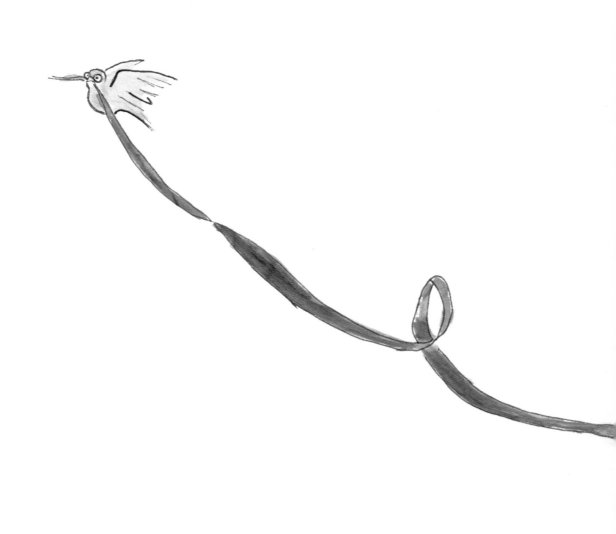

"Hope is the thing with feathers
That perches in the soul,
And sings the tune without the words,
And never stops at all."
—Emily Dickinson

Written by:
CARRIE J.

Carrie earned a BA in English and then went on to spend many years working in the creative realms of both fashion and film. Through her work, she found herself increasingly devoted to characterization, and creating a compelling story-behind-the-story in each of her projects. She is thrilled to be able to bring this same passion and devotion to the playful, imaginative world of writing children's books, as well as creatively directing the Hope and Whimsy Co brand. Born in the Deep South, Carrie has transplanted her Georgian roots numerous times living on both east and west coasts, but has currently settled them in the rocky soil of Central Oregon. She now lives on a farm with her husband, four young children, a stubborn mare and cheeky mini pony, and a lovable cat and Labrador. When she isn't working on her next children's book, her time is swallowed whole by a great big beautiful Life of children, farm life, laundry, and trying very hard (but not super successfully) to grow things.

@lovecarriej | www.hopeandwhimsyco.com

Illustrated by:

KAMDON CALLAWAY

Kamdon lives in the bustling mountain town of Bend, Oregon. She shares her home, she lovingly calls "The Ranch," with her two children, four dogs, and three chickens. With a BFA in art, and an extensive, wide-ranging portfolio of art projects under her belt, she recently transitioned from being a stay-at-home mom, to a full-time professional artist. Illustrating children's books is one of her greatest joys, as it utilizes her love and talent for taking the mere essence of an idea and translating that into living, breathing splashes of vivid, whimsical tale! When Kamdon isn't designing or illustrating in her studio, you will still likely find her covered in paint--or fabric swatches, or cake icing--as her desire to Create is an ongoing, daily matter of importance to her. (Tidiness, however, is not.)

@kamdonkreations | www.kamdonkreations.com

GLOSSARY

Ablaze: like fire in color.

Admire, Admired, Admiration: to have a high opinion of; respect. to look at with delight, wonder, and approval.

Affect, Affected: to imitate or pretend to have.

Agile: moving quickly and gracefully.

Air: the way a thing or person appears to be.

Amble, Ambled: to walk at a slow, easy pace.

Amuse, Amused: to hold the interest of in a pleasant way; entertain.

Animate, Animated: to bring to life.

Anticipation: the condition of expecting or hoping.

Ashamed: feeling shame or guilt for doing something wrong or foolish.

Askew: not straight.

Assure, Assured: to cause to feel certain or secure.

Astound, Astounded: to cause surprise or wonder; amaze.

Attentive, Attentiveness: paying close attention. paying attention to the needs or comfort of others.

Awe: a very strong feeling of wonder mixed with respect or fear.

Beam, Beaming: to smile widely or happily.

Belong, Belonging: to be accepted as part of a group; fit in.

Betray, Betrayal: to not be loyal or faithful to.

Bizarre: strikingly odd or unusual, esp. in appearance or behavior.

Bliss, Blissful: very great happiness.

Bluster, Blustery: to blow in a strong and noisy way.

Boast: to talk with too much pride; brag.

Bold: brave; daring. easy to notice; attracting attention.

Buoy: a float used to prevent someone from drowning. to cause to float (often followed by "up").

Burden: something that is carried or difficult to bear.

Camaraderie: friendship, good humor, and closeness among a group; comradeship.

Character: all those things that make a person, place, or thing different from others. strong moral qualities.

Cherish, Cherished: to value with great love and care.

Community: a particular area where a group of people live. a group of people who live close together or have shared interests.

Compassion: a feeling of sharing another's suffering that leads to a desire to help.

Compel, Compelled: to force or drive to do something.

Consistent: having a regular style or pattern; not changing.

Constancy: the quality of being constant or invariable, as in purpose, opinion, or devotion; steadfastness; loyalty.

Constant, Constantly: going on without a pause; persistent. constantly: all the time; without stopping.

Contented, Contentedly: satisfied with things as they are; content.

Contort, Contorted: to twist into an unusual or unnatural shape. to become twisted into an unusual or unnatural shape.

Determination, Determined: the quality of having a firm goal or being determined.

Disastrous: causing grave harm, loss, ruin, or the like; tragic or calamitous.

Disdain: to regard or treat with contempt; scorn.

Dispel: to scatter or drive away in all directions.

Distinguish, Distinguished: to tell apart by seeing differences (often followed by "from"). to act in a way that draws special recognition or distinction.

Distort, Distorted: to twist out of shape; change the way a thing looks or acts.

Earnest: having or showing a serious manner. honestly concerned or sincere.

Efficient: operating or working in a way that gets results, with little wasted effort.

Elaborate: planned or carried out with great care and attention to details.

Encouraging: arousing feelings of hope or courage. tending to give help, support, or approval.

Enthusiasm: a strong interest in something.

Enthusiastic: having or showing great interest.

Faithful, Faithfully, Faithfulness: able to be trusted or relied on.

Forlorn: desolate or unhappy, as from abandonment or weariness.

Gallantly: brave and dashing.

Garish: marked by excessive or tasteless color or decoration; gaudy; flashy.

Graciously: likely to do what is polite, kind, or right.

Harry, Harried: to attack or annoy repeatedly or constantly; harass.

Hideous: looking very ugly or frightening; disgusting.

Honor, Honored, Honoring: to show respect or admiration for. to give a special award or recognition to.

Impact, Impacted: a strong and powerful effect.

Impromptu: thought of, made, or done without plan, preparation, or practice; spontaneous or improvised.

Indifference: lack of interest, esp. when interest is called for, expected, or hoped for.

Integrity: a strong sense of honesty; firmness of moral character.

Intent, Intently: very concentrated in attention; focused.

Intricate, Intricately: having many complex parts, angles, or aspects; involved; elaborate.

Jeer: to remark in a loud, mocking, abusive manner.

Jibe: to make mocking or derisive comments.

Lanky: tall, thin, and awkward.

Lilting: a pleasing variation in musical tone or rhythm.

Lithe: characterized by light, graceful, flexible movements.

Loon: a large black and white water bird with a call that sounds like a loud laugh.

Loyal: showing devotion and faithfulness to someone or something.

Magenta: the color that comes from mixing red and purple paint.

Magnificent: very grand in size or splendid in beauty.

Manipulate, Manipulated: to handle or operate skillfully with the hands.

Meandered: to wander in speech or movement without a goal or direction.

Mesmerized, Mesmerizing: to hold the attention or compel the obedience of, as though by hypnotism; fascinate; enthrall.

Mock, Mocked, Mocking: to make fun of in a mean way.

Outrageous: shocking in behavior, appearance, or speech.

Patient: able to stand trouble or pain without complaining.

Peace, Peaceful: a state of quiet or calm.

Persevere: to continue steadfastly in a task or course of action or hold steadfastly to a belief or commitment, esp. when met with opposition or difficulties; persist.

Phenomenon: an unusual or remarkable person or event.

Poise: the ability to act in a calm and confident manner.

Preen, Preened: to show or have great pride and satisfaction in (oneself).

Pristine: pure, fresh, or clean as new; unspoiled or unsullied.

Profuse, Profusely: given in a generous way.

Putrid: having a strong unpleasant odor, as of decaying matter.

Quaint: pleasant in an old-fashioned way.

Regatta: a boat race or planned series of such races, esp. of sailing vessels.

Remorse: a feeling of guilt and real sorrow over having done something wrong.

Repulsive: prompting disgust or aversion; distasteful.

Respect: the state or condition of being thought of with honor or admiration; such admiration itself.

Revulsion: violent dislike and disgust; abhorrence; loathing.

Roe: a small deer found in Europe and Asia.

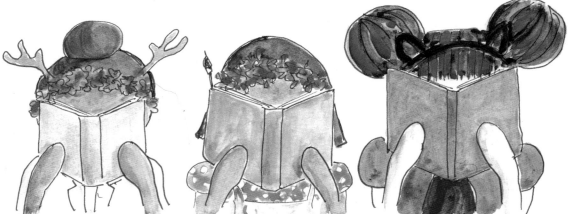

Sarcasm, Sarcastic: the use of scornful or mocking remarks.

Saunter, Sauntered: to walk at an unhurried, leisurely pace; stroll.

Seethe, Seething: to boil or bubble.

Sneer, Sneering: a look on the face that expresses scorn or lack of respect.

Soiree: a party or social gathering held in the evening.

Somali: any of a type of domestic cat developed from the Abyssinian cat.

Steadfast: able to be trusted or relied on; loyal. not likely to change; firmly in place.

Taunt, Taunting: to make fun of, tease, or challenge using mean language.

Tender, Tenderly: showing love or kindness in a gentle way.

Ticker-tape: paper tape upon which a telegraphic ticker prints stock quotations, reports, and the like.

Translucent: letting only some light through so that what can be seen on the other side is not clear.

Tress, Tresses: a woman's or girl's locks or curls of hair, usu. long and unbound.

Trivial: not valuable or important; insignificant.

Trustworthy: worthy or deserving of trust and confidence; steadily dependable; reliable.

Unique: being the only one of its type; sole; single. having no equal; different from everything else.

Unpredictable: not predictable; not able to be known beforehand.

Unwavering, Unwaveringly: steady; not moving back and forth or changing positions.

Upscale: costly or stylish.

Viable: capable of being put into effect; practicable.

Vivid: able to invent or form strong, clear images.

Vulnerable, Vulnerability: able to be hurt or injured.

Ward: a child or other person who has been placed under control of a person or group other than a parent by a court of law.

Whimsical: slightly odd or amusing in a uniquely imaginative way; fanciful; quaint.

CHARACTER QUALITIES

"For me, these special words
hold so much more meaning and depth
than dictionaries can provide.
Since many of them are central themes
that thread their way throughout the book,
I wanted to write them
in a more meaningful, applicable way.
My mama and I worked together on writing them,
and while they may not be perfect,
I hope the hearts of them are felt and understood."

—Carrie J.

Compassionate

Caring enough to recognize and share others' pain, and doing all you can to help meet their needs.

Contentment

Having the wisdom to recognize that all you currently have is all you need. Feeling deeply thankful and at peace with what you've been given.

Courageous

Having the strength to do or say something to help others or yourself, even if you're afraid.

Encouraging

Making others feel hopeful, valued, or unafraid by your words or actions.

Faithful

Consistently choosing to do what is right, and fully committing to follow through on promises, even if it means making great sacrifices to do so.

Forgiving

Not keeping a record of wrongs for those that have hurt or angered you. Having a settled peace in your heart, and showing grace to others.

Friendship
A special relationship between friends that involves trust, love, loyalty, patience, compassion, understanding, humility, forgiveness, grace, joy, and general silliness. True friendships have an abundance of these qualities, which should be displayed by all involved in the friendship (true friendship is never one-sided).

Generous
Giving freely with a joyful heart without an expectation of receiving anything in return.

Grace
Demonstrating patience, kindness, understanding, and forgiveness toward others—even to those that hurt you or dislike you.

Gracious
Generously kind and considerate. Happy to serve others and make them feel welcome, and at ease.

Grateful
Expressing thankfulness and joy, with a humble spirit, through your words or actions.

Honor
Showing someone by words or actions that they are of great value, worth, and importance.

Hope
A feeling of soaring joy that comes from fully believing and expecting that good things will happen for either yourself or others.

Humble
Having a wise, mature perspective and a grateful spirit. Quietly confident, but not prideful or arrogant. Having a genuine desire to serve, help, and praise others.

Integrity
Faithfully doing what is right and honest—even when nobody is looking. Having a clean, pure heart.

Joyful
Expressing abundant joy or gladness from a grateful heart.

Kind
Showing friendliness and graciousness in gentle, generous ways. Showing others they are valued by you.

Love

Caring for and valuing others more than yourself. It is the opposite of selfishness. "Love bears all things, believes all things, hopes all things, endures all things." I Corinthians 13:7

Loyal

Loving or serving someone at all times, no matter what.

Patient

Calmly waiting without complaint, with a thankful heart—even during hard times.

Respectful

Showing others that you value them, even if you don't agree with them.

Selfless

Showing others that you love and value them more than yourself by putting their needs or desires ahead of your own.

Trustworthy

Consistently keeping your word, showing respect to others by what you choose to do and say—and by what you choose not to do or say—and faithfully doing what is right.